THE LIFE OF
LEONARDO DA VINCI

By
Susie Hodge

School Specialty®
Publishing

Columbus, Ohio

THE CAST

Leonardo da Vinci *1452–1519. Da Vinci was born on April 15, 1452, in Vinci, Italy. He grew up to be a great inventor, scientist, military engineer, philosopher, botanist, and mathematician, as well as a brilliant painter and sculptor. Many of his inventions were ahead of their time. Leonardo lived and worked for kings and dukes and was accepted, then and now, as a genius. He died in France on May 2, 1519, at the age of 68.*

Andrea del Verrocchio *1435–1488. Verrocchio was born in Florence, Italy. He became an extremely successful sculptor and painter and taught some of the greatest artists of the Renaissance, including Leonardo da Vinci. He died in Venice in 1488, when he was 53.*

Michelangelo Buonarroti *1475–1564. Michelangelo was born in Caprese, Italy on March 6, 1475. He was a sculptor, painter, architect, and poet and was Leonardo's greatest artistic rival. Like da Vinci, Michelangelo became famous and was considered a genius even during his lifetime. He died in Rome on February 18, 1564, when he was 89 years old.*

Raphael Sanzio *1483–1520. Raphael was born on April 6, 1483, in Urbino, Italy. His father was also a painter and poet. Raphael admired Leonardo and Michelangelo, but they resented him. He died on his 37th birthday in 1520.*

Duke Ludovico Sforza *1452–1507. Sforza was born on July 27, 1452. He was the Duke of Milan for only five years, from 1494 to 1500, but he ruled the city in his nephew's name for longer. Sforza was Leonardo da Vinci's first parton. He died on May 27, 1507, a prisoner in the castle of Loches, France. His castle, Castello Sforzesco, still stands in Milan.*

Pope Leo X *1475–1513. The pope was born Giovanni di Lorenzo de Medici on December 11, 1475, in Florence, Italy. His family was the most powerful in Florence at the time. Leo X was pope from 1513 until his death eight years later on December 1, 1521, in Rome.*

School Specialty Publishing

Copyright © ticktock Entertainment Ltd. 2006 First published in Great Britain in 2006 by ticktock Media Ltd., Unit 2, Orchard Business Centre, North Farm Road, Tunbridge Wells, Kent, TN2 3XF. This edition published in 2006 by School Specialty Publishing, a member of the School Specialty Family. Send all inquiries to School Specialty Publishing, 8720 Orion Place, Columbus, OH 43240.

Hardback ISBN 0-7696-4718-9 Paperback ISBN 0-7696-4698-0
1 2 3 4 5 6 7 8 9 10 TTM 10 09 08 07 06
Printed in China.

CONTENTS

SETTING THE SCENE

A time of intense focus on learning and creative expression, the Renaissance in Italy during the 15th century brought along many improvements in art, poetry, printing, math, and other areas of the arts and sciences. Leonardo da Vinci was a painter, astronomer, sculptor, geologist, mathematician, botanist, animal behaviorist, inventor, engineer, architect, and musician. Throughout his long career, Leonardo worked for kings, popes, and dukes. He traveled and worked in Florence, Milan, Mantua, Rome, Venice, Pavia, Bologna, and France. Not only did he paint pictures like *The Mona Lisa*, he also invented designs for a helicopter, a mechanical loom, a car, a bike, and a multi-barreled gun.

DUCH
OF
SAVO

F R A N C E

Florence, one of the cultural capitals of Italy in the 15th century

Italy in the 15th century was not the united country it is today. At that time, it was divided into many small independent states. There were rulers in each of these states. They fought wars against each other and against smaller neighboring states to increase their power.

A - March of Montferrat

B - County of Asti

C - Republic of Lucca

D - Duchy of Modena

E - Duchy of Mantua

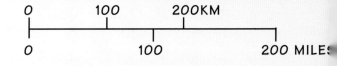

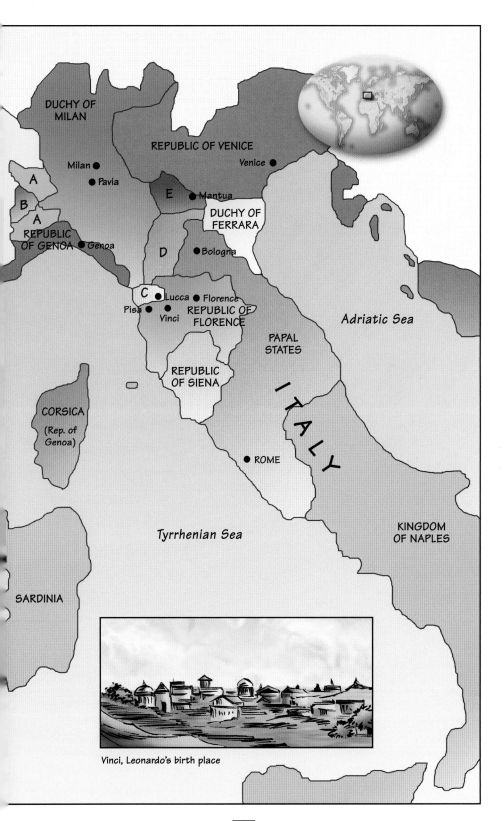

DUCHY OF
MILAN

REPUBLIC OF VENICE

Milan ●

Venice ●

A

● Pavia

B

A

E

● Mantua

DUCHY OF
FERRARA

REPUBLIC
OF GENOA ● Genoa

D

● Bologna

C

Lucca ●

● Florence

Pisa ●

●

Vinci

REPUBLIC OF
FLORENCE

Adriatic Sea

PAPAL
STATES

REPUBLIC OF
SIENA

CORSICA

(Rep. of
Genoa)

● ROME

Tyrrhenian Sea

KINGDOM
OF NAPLES

SARDINIA

Vinci, Leonardo's birth place

A YOUNG ARTIST

Leonardo was born near Vinci, in the countryside of Tuscany, Italy, in April 1452. His mother, Caterina, was a young peasant woman. His father, Ser Piero, was from a fairly wealthy family. They did not marry, but they were both proud of their baby. Caterina kept Leonardo with her while he was a baby, and Ser Piero visited them often.

That's the city of Florence, Leonardo. We have a house there, too, my son. You will soon move there with your stepmother and me.

When Leonardo was two years old, his father took him to live in his family's country house. There, he became close to his grandfather and his uncle. Ser Piero soon married a wealthy young woman from Florence.

Leonardo loved his father's brother, Francesco, and followed him around, always asking questions. Francesco loved Leonardo and told him all he knew.

You need to understand the countryside, Leonardo. Then, you can help me in the fields!

Of course I will help you, Uncle Francesco!

Leonardo showed an interest in many things.

Look, Dad, here are my ideas!

You are very clever, my boy. Although you cannot follow me in my work. I will see that you have the best teachers in Florence.

FAST FACT The Renaissance was a period in history when European scholars were inspired with new ideas after the rediscovery of ancient Greece and Rome.

Florence was an exciting place to be. New and innovative buildings were being built, and most of the best artists in Europe worked there.

Verrocchio, what do you think of my son's artistic abilities?

I've never seen such talent in an untrained boy. One day, he will be a greater artist than I. He can certainly come and learn with me.

When Leonardo was 14, Ser Piero took him to the workshop, called a *bottega*, of the famous artist, Andrea del Verrocchio.

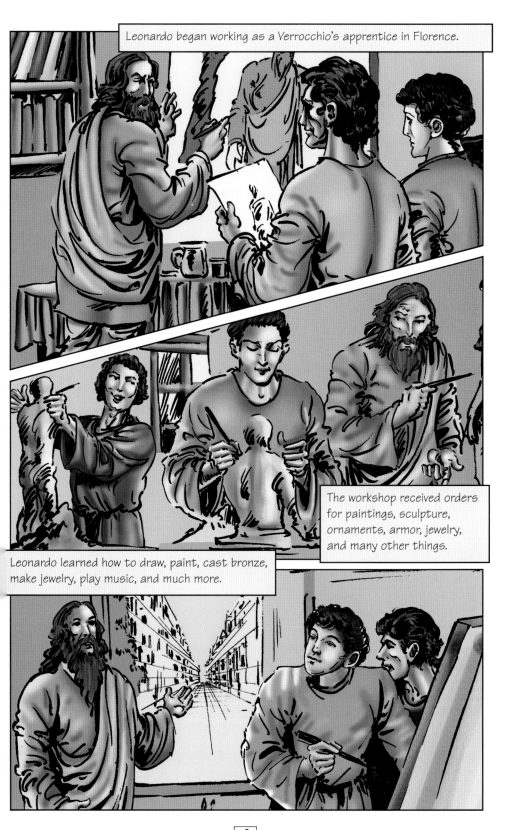

Leonardo began working as a Verrocchio's apprentice in Florence.

The workshop received orders for paintings, sculpture, ornaments, armor, jewelry, and many other things.

Leonardo learned how to draw, paint, cast bronze, make jewelry, play music, and much more.

In the fifteenth century, Florence was particularly lively. Scholars, philosophers, and artists came to discuss their ideas. There were workshops of all kinds, and people played music and strolled through the streets.

Any requests?

Keep still, Leonardo! I've nearly finished.

They're making me laugh!

Yes, play that song again, so we can sing the chorus this time.

Sometimes, Leonardo was Verrocchio's model.

Leonardo learned to sing and play the lute.

Often, other artists would come to the workshop to discuss ideas with Verrocchio and his apprentices.

So, the new way of mixing paint is using oil?

Yes, but I prefer tempera, although Leonardo says oil blends more easily.

When Verrocchio had a large piece of art to produce, all the apprentices worked on it.

Come, we must finish this painting of Tobias and the Angel today!

Ok, I'll paint the little dog.

FAST FACT From medieval times, people in various trades grouped together in associations, or guilds. These groups decided on rules for their trades and set prices for their services.

Leonardo often spoke to teachers of science, mathematics, and philosophy.

How does illness enter our bodies?

So many questions! We don't have all the answers, but perhaps one day you will find out.

One day, Leonardo and two of the other apprentices, Botticelli and Credi, were helping Verrocchio with his painting of *The Baptism of Christ*.

I'm just finishing - what's wrong, master?

Leonardo, I knew this would happen. You are a far greater artist than I will ever be. I will never again raise a paintbrush.

It was stimulating to be in Florence at that time. Wealthy merchants and bankers paid for architects to build innovative new buildings. With Leonardo's thirst for knowledge, it was the perfect place for him to be.

In 1472, he became a master craftsman of his trade. He had earned the right to be called master.

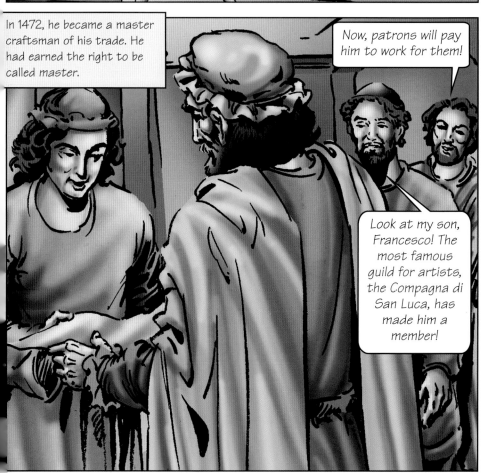

Now, patrons will pay him to work for them!

Look at my son, Francesco! The most famous guild for artists, the Compagna di San Luca, has made him a member!

Officially a master, Leonardo opened his own workshop in 1476. However, he continued to work with Verocchio until 1477. Leonardo's paintings, sculptures, and metalwork astonished people; they had never seen such realistic work. In his spare time, he drew and painted whatever and whenever he could, producing the kind of art that no one had seen before.

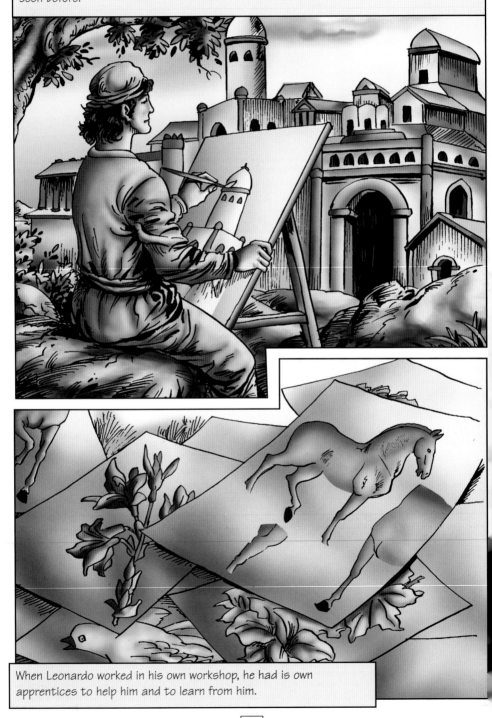

When Leonardo worked in his own workshop, he had is own apprentices to help him and to learn from him.

Sometimes, Leonardo's paintings looked so convincingly realistic that people thought they were real.

Mix up some more of that red paint, please.

At last, my reputation is growing. Once the Medicis pay me, everyone will want my work!

So, young man, we have seen your work. We want you to work for us.

The powerful Medici family asked him to their magnificent home.

FAST FACT The Medici family was made up of powerful, wealthy, and feared merchants and bankers. They ruled Florence between 1434 and 1737, encouraging art, architecture, music, and scholarship.

15

A MAN OF MANY TALENTS

Although Leonardo was running a successful workshop in Florence, he went to Milan in 1482 to meet the powerful Ludovico Sforza.

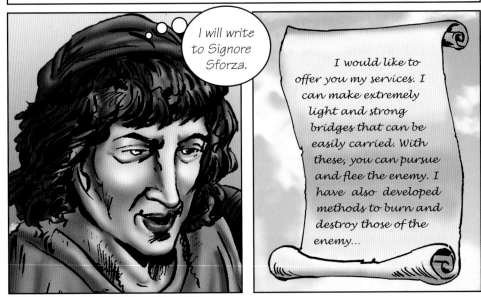

I will write to Signore Sforza.

I would like to offer you my services. I can make extremely light and strong bridges that can be easily carried. With these, you can pursue and flee the enemy. I have also developed methods to burn and destroy those of the enemy...

He also created a silver lute to impress his wealthy patron.

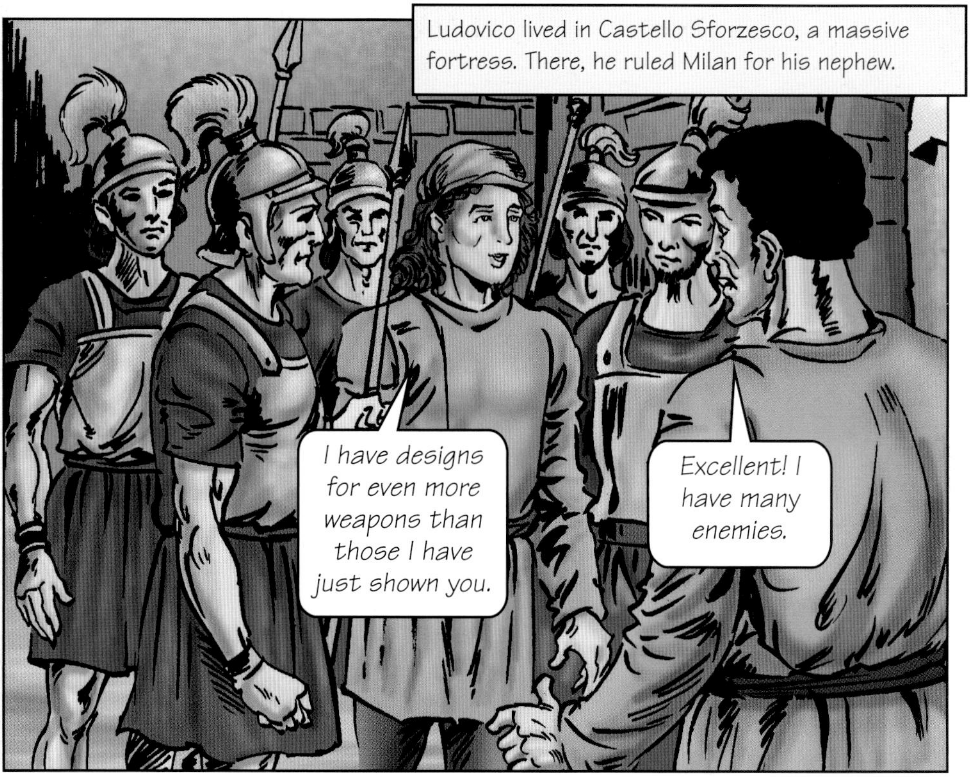
Ludovico lived in Castello Sforzesco, a massive fortress. There, he ruled Milan for his nephew.
I have designs for even more weapons than those I have just shown you.
Excellent! I have many enemies.

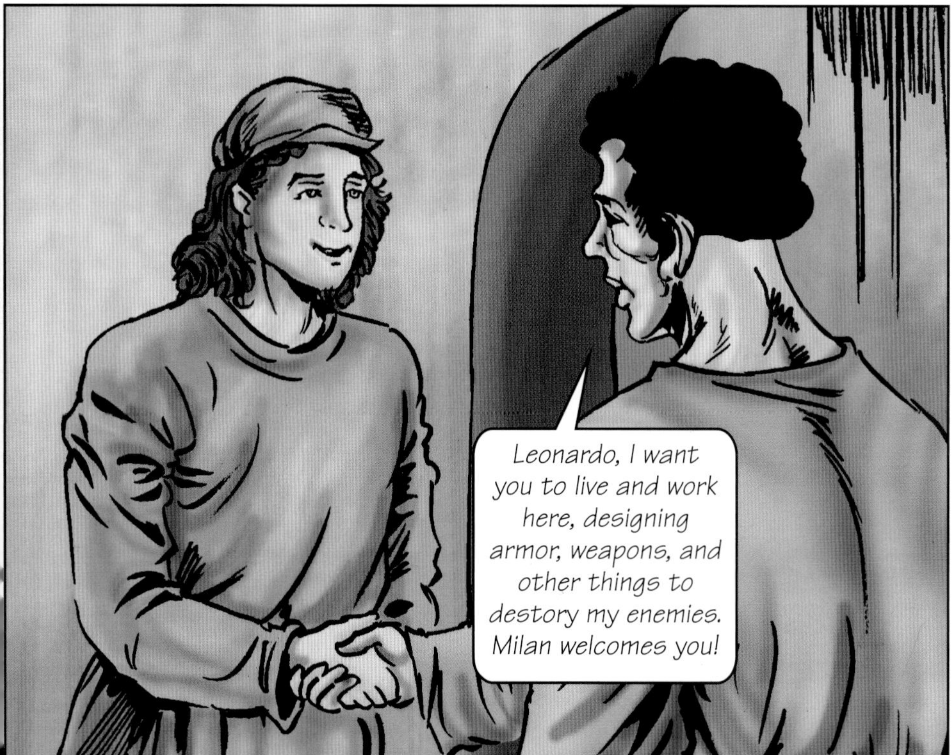
Leonardo, I want you to live and work here, designing armor, weapons, and other things to destory my enemies. Milan welcomes you!

Thank you. I will be able to work well here!

This will be your studio. Make yourself at home, and let me know whatever you need.

You seem like you will be a quick learner. You can be my apprentice, Salaí.

As the weeks and months passed, Leonardo designed many things for Ludovico, including weapons, buildings, bridges, and more.

He designed an armored tank.

He also designed a multi-barreled gun.

Leonardo developed techniques to create shadows in his paintings.

Leonardo found a place to live with the Predis brothers, who were also artists.

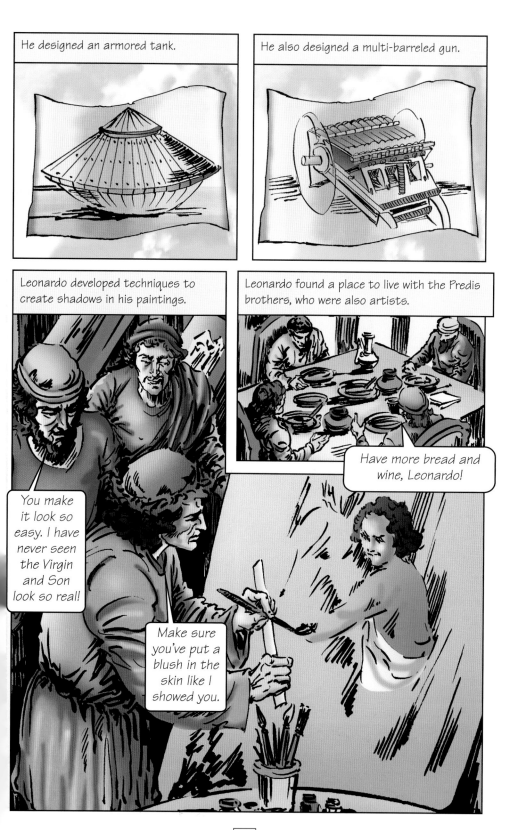

Have more bread and wine, Leonardo!

You make it look so easy. I have never seen the Virgin and Son look so real!

Make sure you've put a blush in the skin like I showed you.

Even while he was working for Duke Ludovico, Leonardo didn't stop investigating and inventing. Although he hated war, he was being paid well to design the most dangerous weapons.

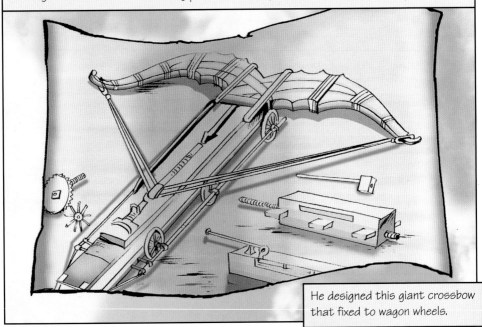

He designed this giant crossbow that fixed to wagon wheels.

The narrow streets of Milan are dirty. Many people are dying of the plague. This is my design for an ideal city that will banish dirt and disease.

The world can only be learned through studying everything closely and thinking about it. Many of Leonardo's sketches revealed this.

Leonardo was fascinated by beauty, but he also drew many funny and grotesque pictures.

Leonardo opened another workshop in Milan called the *Accademia Leonardi Vinci.*

Leonardo was so busy that he had five apprentices. He loved to tell jokes and stories to people who visited his studio.

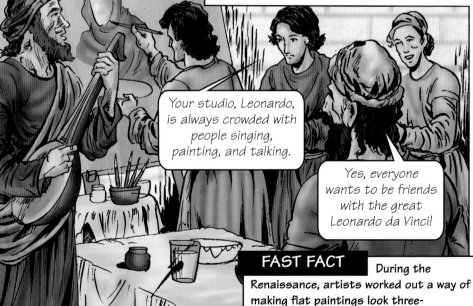

Your studio, Leonardo, is always crowded with people singing, painting, and talking.

Yes, everyone wants to be friends with the great Leonardo da Vinci!

FAST FACT During the Renaissance, artists worked out a way of making flat paintings look three-dimensional. Leonardo used this technique in his paintings, drawings, and designs. It was called *linear perspective.*

One day, Duke Sforza gave Leonardo a great commission. With 80 tons of bronze, Leonardo could create a very grand statue.

The bronze monument was for Ludovico's father, Francesco Sforza. Leonardo made many sketches of horses and monuments. It took nearly ten years of preparation!

So you see, Duke, your statue will be a rearing horse, 23 feet tall.

I like it!

Before Leonardo could complete his statue, French troops marched into Italy.

The bronze was used to make cannons, and the French troops later destroyed da Vinci's clay model of the horse as target practice.

SCIENTIST AND MATHEMATICIAN

Leonardo da Vinci's curiosity knew no bounds. He dissected corpses so that he could study how the human body works.

Through his studies, he learned many things about the body that had not been understood before.

He also watched operations. It was the first time in history that the body became an object of serious scientific research.

With the help of someone who worked in the hospital, Leonardo took corpses of people to examine in his studio.

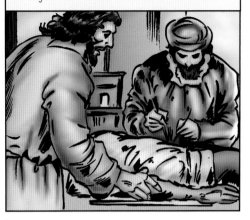

Leonardo was kept busy with many projects for Ludovico, including creating the set for "Feast of Paradise," a play in honor of Ludovico's nephew's marriage to the king of Naples' granddaughter.

FAST FACT Doctors were only just starting to realize that the best way to learn about how the body works was to look inside.

Leonardo made friends with the mathematician Luca Pacioli, a Franciscan friar. Pacioli taught Leonardo about mathematics. In return, Leonardo illustrated Pacioli's book about proportion.

My drawing, The Vitruvian Man, is based on the work of the ancient Roman architect Vitruvius. It shows the proportions of the human body perfectly.

In 1495, Leonardo was asked to paint *The Last Supper*, a huge mural of Jesus and the apostles, at a monastery in Milan.

I've invented a new technique so I can brush paint directly on the wall, making the colors brighter. I used mathematics to compose this 33-foot long picture. I've broken with tradition by putting the traitor Judas in with all the other disciples. It's turning out well, but the monks who are paying for it are angry because it's taking so long.

In 1499, when the French took control of Milan, Leonardo left with Pacioli, Salaì, and his other apprentices. Times were changing for the great artist.

WAR AND WATER

At first, Leonardo, Pacioli, Salaí, and the apprentices went to Mantua. Then, they traveled to Venice.

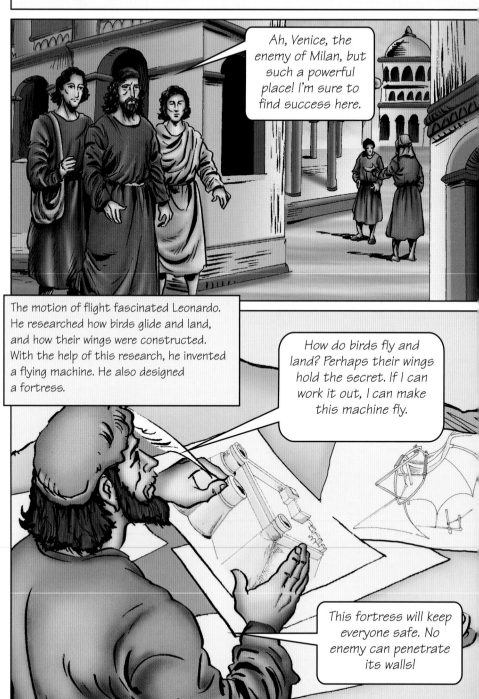

Ah, Venice, the enemy of Milan, but such a powerful place! I'm sure to find success here.

The motion of flight fascinated Leonardo. He researched how birds glide and land, and how their wings were constructed. With the help of this research, he invented a flying machine. He also designed a fortress.

How do birds fly and land? Perhaps their wings hold the secret. If I can work it out, I can make this machine fly.

This fortress will keep everyone safe. No enemy can penetrate its walls!

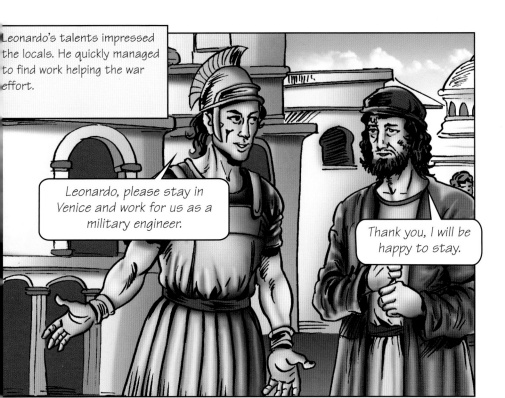

Leonardo's talents impressed the locals. He quickly managed to find work helping the war effort.

Leonardo, please stay in Venice and work for us as a military engineer.

Thank you, I will be happy to stay.

Venice was under threat of an attack by the Ottoman Empire. When Leonardo moved there, Ottoman warships were off the coast, waiting to invade.

FAST FACT The Ottoman Empire was based in present-day Turkey. Ottoman sultans had captured many Christian lands, and now wanted Venice, too.

Leonardo worked on many plans to thwart an Ottoman invasion

With this wooden dam, we can flood the Ottomans Then, they'll either drown or flee and never return.

Leonardo then went on to design a submarine, a deep-sea diving suit, and a breathing apparatus to allow soldiers to walk under water.

Leonardo, this is marvelous! No man will be able to fight against your brilliant designs!

After a few months, Leonardo and his friends returned to Florence. He spent time with his father, who was now married to his fourth wife.

Great to see you, my son. Things have changed around here. The Medicis are no longer in power.

I had heard, yet for all my success, I still need patrons.

The people of Florence were pleased to have Leonardo back. In 1502, the cunning and feared military ruler Cesare Borgia came to see him.

Leonardo, will you work for me as an architect and engineer?

Of course!

Leonardo traveled with Cesare throughout Italy, studying how cities and their buildings were designed.

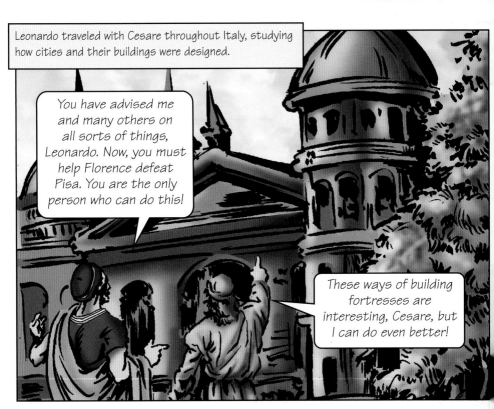

You have advised me and many others on all sorts of things, Leonardo. Now, you must help Florence defeat Pisa. You are the only person who can do this!

These ways of building fortresses are interesting, Cesare, but I can do even better!

This is how we could redirect the Arno River to prevent the people of Pisa from getting to the sea. Here is a canal that will allow Florence's people access to the sea, instead!

Genius!

Leonardo met Niccolo Machiavelli, second chancellor to Florence. Machiavelli and Leonardo respected each other's intelligence and became friends. They worked together on some of Leonardo's inventions and ideas.

It is good to meet you, Leonardo.

I am honored to meet the well-known writer and philospher, Niccolo Machiavelli.

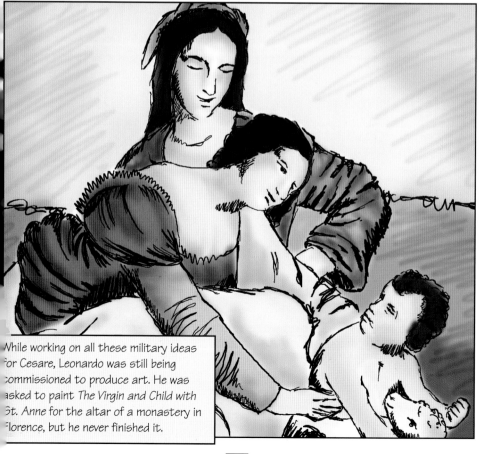

While working on all these military ideas for Cesare, Leonardo was still being commissioned to produce art. He was asked to paint *The Virgin and Child with St. Anne* for the altar of a monastery in Florence, but he never finished it.

MAPS AND THE MONA LISA

Using a magnetic compass and his knowledge of mathematics, Leonardo made accurate maps of many places. He was one of the first people to do accurate maps.

Leonardo was famous for painting beautiful portraits for many wealthy people in Florence.

In 1503, Florence commissioned both Michelangelo and da Vinci to paint a battle scene at the Palazzo Vecchio. The two artists and their apprentices kept out of each other's way.

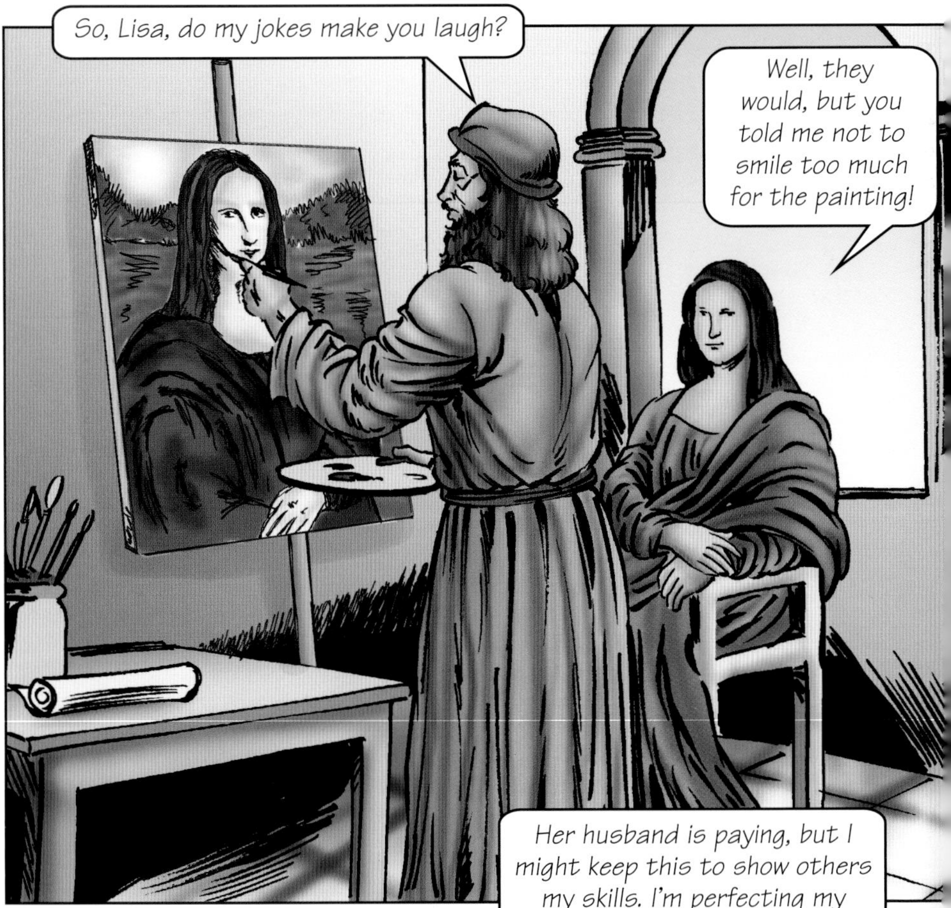
So, Lisa, do my jokes make you laugh?
Well, they would, but you told me not to smile too much for the painting!

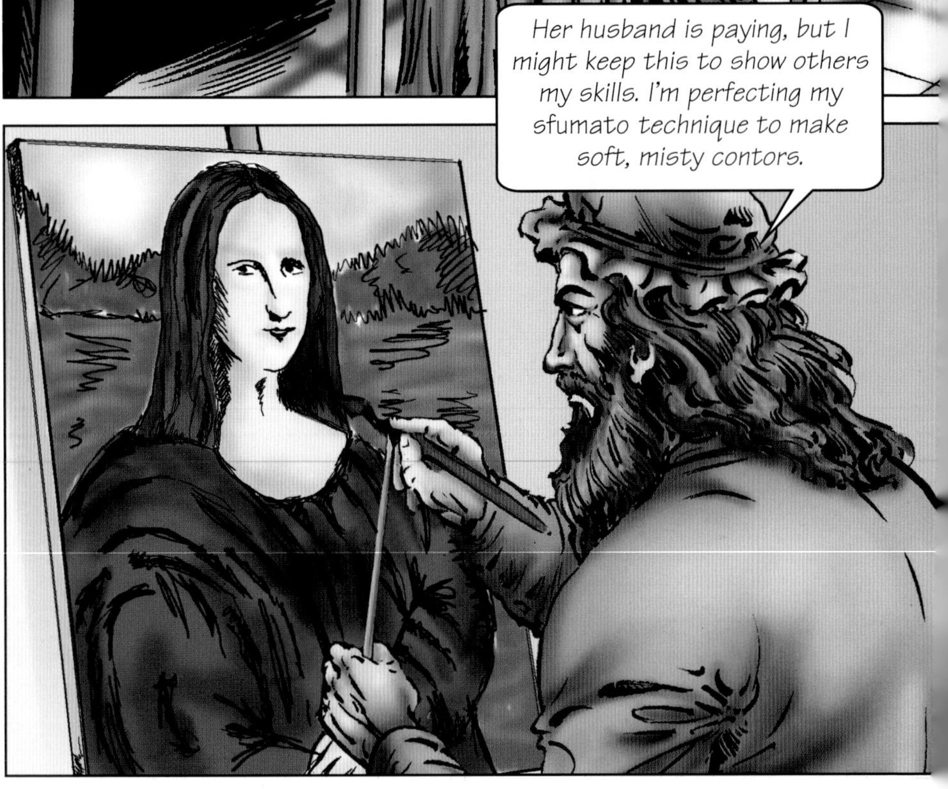
Her husband is paying, but I might keep this to show others my skills. I'm perfecting my sfumato technique to make soft, misty contors.

The printing press had recently been invented. Now, books could be printed and bought fairly easily. Leonardo could now find and read many books and could also play from sheet music.

Great invention, but I could improve the printing press.

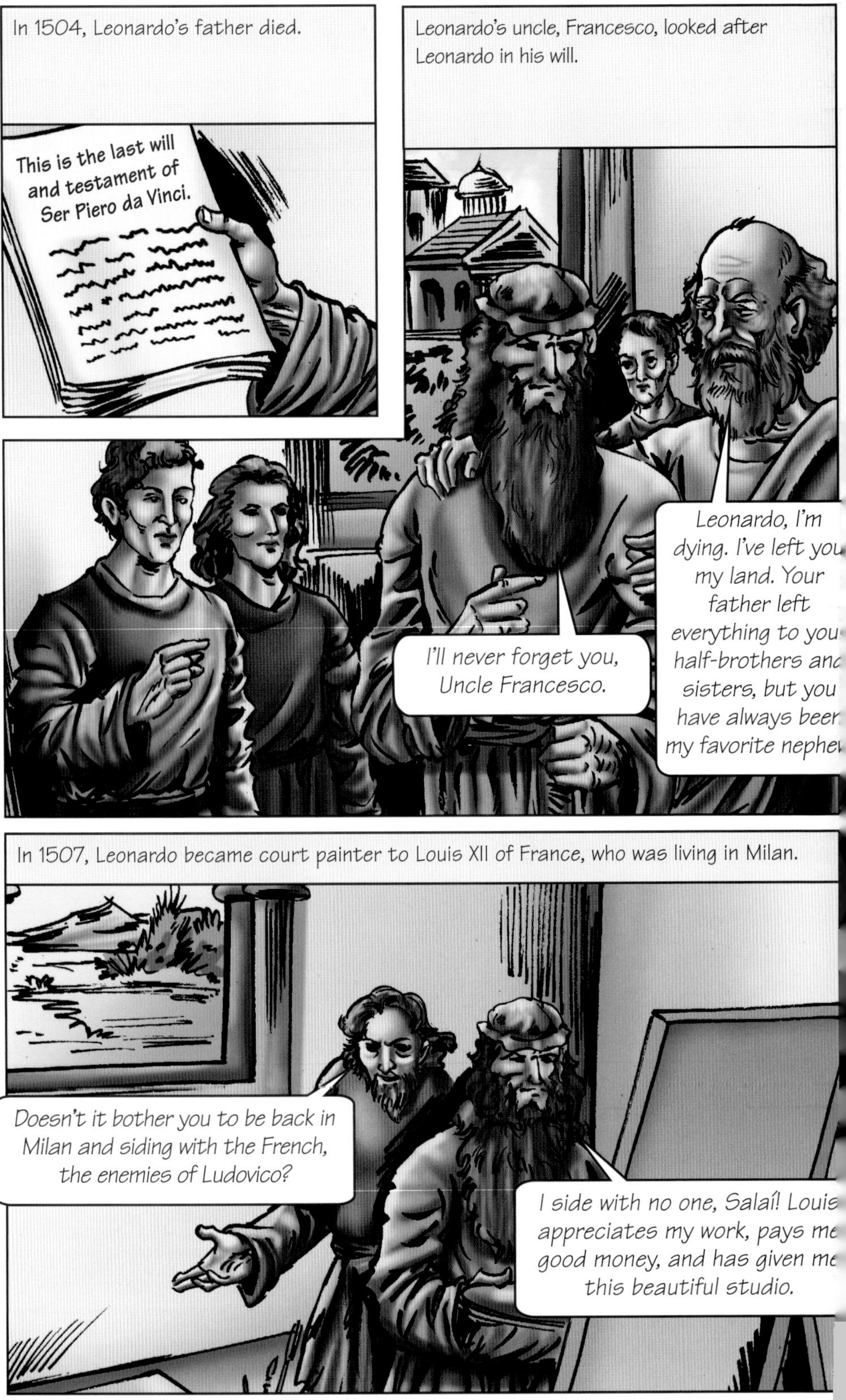

In 1504, Leonardo's father died.
This is the last will and testament of Ser Piero da Vinci.
Leonardo's uncle, Francesco, looked after Leonardo in his will.
Leonardo, I'm dying. I've left yo my land. Your father left everything to you half-brothers an sisters, but you have always bee my favorite nephe
I'll never forget you, Uncle Francesco.
In 1507, Leonardo became court painter to Louis XII of France, who was living in Milan.
Doesn't it bother you to be back in Milan and siding with the French, the enemies of Ludovico?
I side with no one, Salaí! Loui appreciates my work, pays m good money, and has given m this beautiful studio.

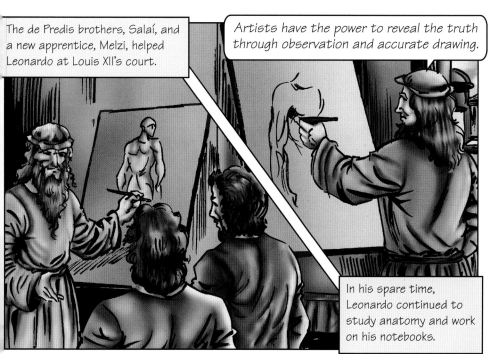

The de Predis brothers, Salaí, and a new apprentice, Melzi, helped Leonardo at Louis XII's court.

Artists have the power to reveal the truth through observation and accurate drawing.

In his spare time, Leonardo continued to study anatomy and work on his notebooks.

I believe that man can fly. Here is one of my designs for a flying machine.

This is very impressive, Leonardo!

FAST FACT Leonardo developed several ideas for flying machines, but they needed materials that only became available 500 years later. His designs were similar to modern gliders, helicopters, and parachutes.

ROME AND FRANCE

In 1513, Ludovico's son drove the French out of Milan, so, once more, Leonardo had no patron. The Medici family no longer ruled Florence, so Leonardo went to Rome, where they were powerful.

Master, are you sure the pope wants you here?

Yes, Melzi. I've been friends with his family for years.

Pope Leo X was a Medici.

All Leonardo's ideas seemed to be ahead of his time.

I believe that Earth is floating in space like all the other planets!

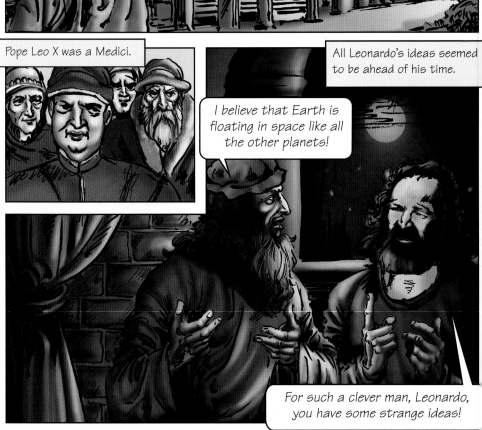

For such a clever man, Leonardo, you have some strange ideas!

Although Leonardo was employed by Pope Leo X, Michelangelo and Raphael—both much younger artists—had been working in Rome for the previous pope. Now, they were also producing amazing works of art for Pope Leo X.

Meanwhile, Leonardo still studied bodies closely to find out how they worked.

Their work is wonderful, but they have learned most of it from me!

Then, Pope Leo X asked Leonardo to produce a religious painting.

My painting of St. John the Baptist will be unlike all previous paintings of him. He will be confident, smiling, and pointing to heaven.

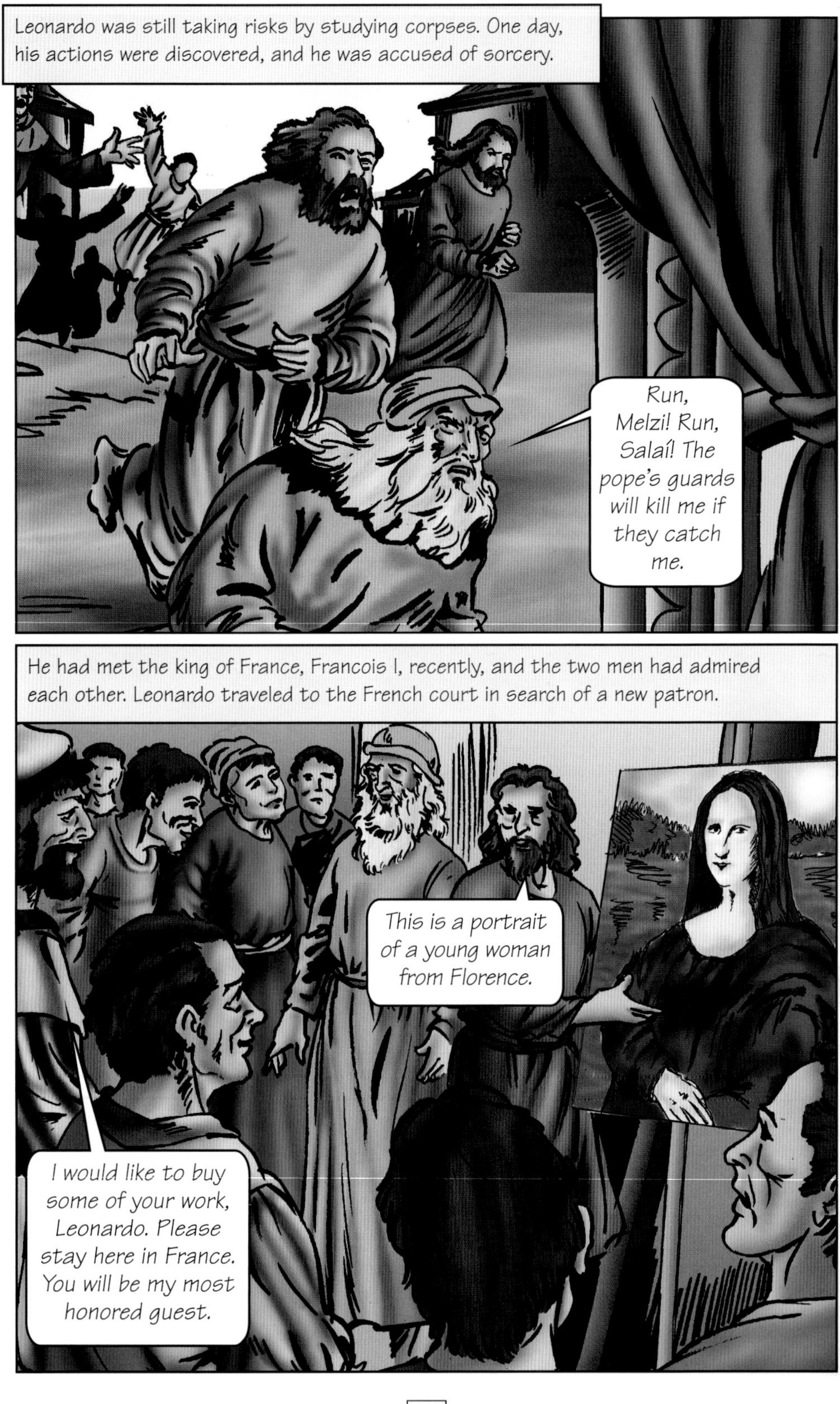
Leonardo was still taking risks by studying corpses. One day, his actions were discovered, and he was accused of sorcery.
Run, Melzi! Run, Salaí! The pope's guards will kill me if they catch me.
He had met the king of France, Francois I, recently, and the two men had admired each other. Leonardo traveled to the French court in search of a new patron.
This is a portrait of a young woman from Florence.
I would like to buy some of your work, Leonardo. Please stay here in France. You will be my most honored guest.

In 1516, Leonardo accepted the French king's invitation to become his chief painter, architect, and mechanic at Amboise in France. By then, Leonardo was 64.

Living happily at the French court, Leonardo continued to fill his notebooks with ideas, plans, and designs.

Leonardo, what will I and the world do without you?

Leonardo had written a will, leaving money and land to Salaí, his half-brothers, and his servants. He left all his books, writings and paintings to Melzi. On May 2, 1519, he died in the arms of his friend, King Francois of France.

I am dying, Francois. Thank you for being such a good friend to me.

Leonardo da Vinci was one of the most famous artists of all time as well as a brilliant inventor. He lived during a time of discovery. Many of his ideas laid the groundwork for later discoveries in anatomy, aeronautics, and engineering.

April 15, 1452: *Leonardo is born in Anchiano, near Vinci to Piero and Caterina.*

1466: *He moves to Florence and enters Verrocchio's workshop.*

1472: *Leonardo joins the artist's guild, the Compagna di San Luca.*

1475: *Michelangelo is born.*

1476: *Leonardo sets up his own workshop. He begins writing notebooks and works for the Medici family.*

1482: *He moves to Milan, leaving the* Adoration of the Magi *unfinished. Leonardo works for Ludovico Sforza as engineer, architect, painter, and sculptor.*

1483: *Raphael is born. Leonardo begins work on* The Virgin of the Rocks.

1489: *Leonardo begins work on a colossal horse statue.*

January 13, 1490: *He draws* The Vitruvian Man *and paints* The Lady with the Ermine.

1495: *Leonardo begins* The Last Supper *in the refectory of the monastery of Santa Maria delle Grazie in Milan.*

1498: *He completes* The Last Supper *and ceiling paintings at Sforzesco Castle in Milan.*

1499: *The French invade Milan and destroy the clay model of Leonardo's giant horse statue. In December, Leonardo travels to Mantua.*

1502: *Cesare Borgia hires him as senior military engineer and architect. Leonardo meets Niccolò Machiavelli.*

1503: *He makes plans to divert the Arno River during the siege of Pisa. Raphael arrives in Florence to study Leonardo's work. Leonardo produces some of the first accurate maps and starts painting* The Mona Lisa.

1504: *His father dies, leaving all his money to Leonardo's nine half-brothers and two half-sisters. Leonardo studies flight and designs a flying machine.*

1506: *Leonardo finishes* The Mona Lisa *and returns to Milan.*

1507: *Uncle Francesco dies, leaving his land to Leonardo. Leonardo becomes the "King's Painter" to Louis XII.*

1508: *Leonardo completes a second version of* The Virgin of the Rocks *and leaves Florence. Michelangelo begins work on the Sistine Ceiling in Rome.*

1513: *He moves to Rome and lives in the Vatican with the new Pope, Leo X.*

1515: *He paints* St. John the Baptist *and makes a mechanical lion for the new French king, Francois I.*

1516: *Leonardo moves to Amboise in France, the court of Francois I.*

1519: *He dies in the company of Francois I, Melzi, and Salai.*

DID YOU KNOW?

1. *Through his parents' various marriages, Leonardo ended up with 17 half brothers and sisters. His mother married and had five more children, and his father* had twelve with other wives.

2. The Last Supper *is carefully proportioned and balanced to show its holiness. Leonardo learned this idea from the ancient Greeks and Romans.*

3. *Leonardo invented a way of painting* The Last Supper *to make the colors extra bright. However, this way of painting made the paint begin to deteriorate almost immediately.*

4. *The invention of the printing press in Leonardo's time immediately helped to spread knowledge, making books available much quicker to more people.*

5. *In the 14th century, China stopped trading with the outside world, so rich merchants spent their money on Italian art rather than buying luxuries from China.*

6. *Many of Leonardo's painted backgrounds include fantastic landscapes and buildings, seen through a veil of mist. This was a technique Leonardo invented, called* sfumato, *or smoky.*

7. *As well as linear perspective, he also used atmospheric, or aerial, perspective to make his backgrounds appear to fade into the distance.*

8. *Throughout his lifetime, Leonardo designed many buildings with great architectural skill and knowledge. However, his designs were constructed much later.*

9. *Although his cathedral and church designs were never constructed, his ideas inspired many later architects.*

10. *Without any military training, Leonardo effectively designed buildings with military reinforcements, cannons, guns, ramps, tanks, and other weapons.*

11. *Leonardo was fascinated by water. He worked out, for example, why shells can sometimes be found on the tops of mountains and how some water comes from underground.*

12. *He learned how a baby grows inside its mother, including the function of the umbilical cord, the womb, and the liquid that surrounds and protects the growing baby.*

13. *Leonardo invented a kind of helicopter, which he called an* airscrew. *He never constructed it, but his theory worked. Modern helicopters are based on the same principle.*

14. *As well as flying machines and helicopters, Leonardo invented the first parachute.*

15. *Leonardo dreamed of machines made for transportation on water, air, and land. One of his inventions was a motor that was a forerunner of the modern car.*

GLOSSARY

Anatomy: *The study of bodies.*

Apprentice: *A young person who is taught by an expert. In the Renaissance, young boys who wanted to become artists trained as apprentices in the workshops of skilled artists.*

Architect: *Someone who designs and plans the construction of buildings.*

Aeronautics: *The design and construction of aircraft.*

Astronomer: *The scientific study of space, planets, and stars.*

Atmospheric or aerial perspective: *A way of creating an image that appears to have depth through the use of color.*

Botanist: *A scientist who studies plants.*

Bottega: *A workshop or studio.*

Canal: *A human-made river used for travel and shipping.*

Cast: *A carved mold used in sculpture.*

Cartoon: *A full-size drawing in preparation for a finished painting.*

Commission: *Paying someone to do work, usually a piece of art.*

Contours: *Outlines of an image.*

Corpse: *The body of a dead person.*

Deteriorate: *To fade or become weaker.*

Disciples: *People who learn from a teacher. In the New Testament, Jesus had twelve disciples.*

Divert: *To send in another direction or re-route.*

Engineer: *Someone who uses science and mathematics to solve problems and produce useful goods.*

Fortress: *A stronghold or castle.*

Geologist: *A scientist who studies the origin, history, and structure of Earth.*

Fresco: *Italian word for* fresh. *In art, it means the technique of applying wet paint to damp, freshly plastered walls so that the painting becomes part of the wall, once the paint and plaster dry.*

Guild: *An association of a trade or craft.*

Innovative: *New, inventive, unique.*

Linear perspective: *A way of creating the appearance of depth by making a painting with a 2D surface appear 3D. Objects appear smaller in the distance.*

Loom: *A machine for weaving.*

Luminous: *Glowing with light.*

Lute: *A stringed, musical instrument.*

Monastery: *Home for a community of monks.*

GLOSSARY

Multi-barrelled gun: *A powerful gun, similar to a machine gun.*

Mural: *A wall painting.*

Palazzo: *Italian word for* grand building *or* palace.

Patron: *A person or group of people who pay someone else to produce something that they want, such as a painting or sculpture.*

Perspective: *Making objects on a 2D surface look 3D. Giving the illusion of depth and distance.*

Philosopher: *A wise person who calmly analyzes and studies life.*

Pigment: *Powdered color that, when mixed with liquid, becomes paint.*

Pope: *The head of the Roman Catholic Church.*

Portrait: *A painting or drawing of a person.*

Redirect: *To send in another direction.*

Renaissance: *During the 14th century, starting in Italy and spreading across Europe, there was a rebirth of learning, creative arts, and ideas. It was not called the* Renaissance *until the 19th century, 500 years after it began.*

Scholars: *People who study and learn.*

Sfumato: *A technique of painting that Leonardo invented, meaning* smoky, *that describes his method of painting soft, blended areas together.*

Ser: *An Italian title similar to* Sir.

Siege: *To block or obstruct. Usually used when a military force blocks entry and exit to a city.*

Signore: *The Italian word for* mister.

Tempera: *Powdered pigment mixed with egg.*

Vitruvian man: *An illustration of a man drawn by Leonardo, using the perfect proportions that the ancient Greek architect Vitruvius had developed.*

Will: *A document that people write, explaining how their money and belongings will be distributed after their deaths.*

Workshop: *A place where work is carried out. In the Renaissance, artists' workshops, called* bottegas, *were where patrons went to commission work and where artists produced the work while training their apprentices.*

INDEX